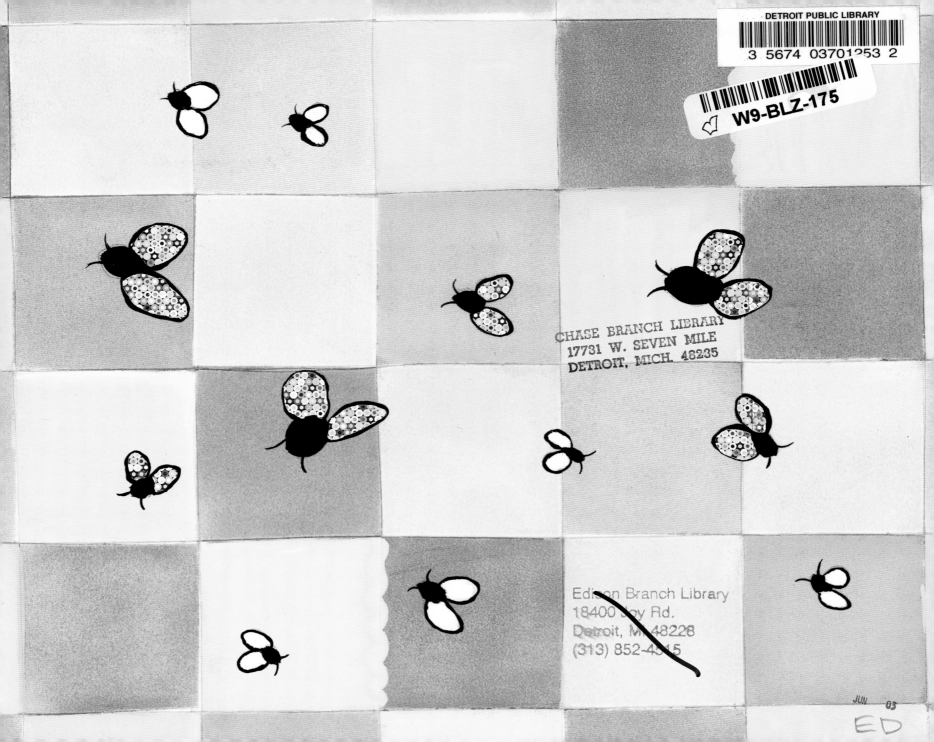

Five green and

and

by Priscilla Burris

speckled FROGS

Cartwheel
·B·O·O·K·S·®

SCHOLASTIC INC.

New York   Toronto   London   Auckland   Sydney   Mexico City
New Delhi   Hong Kong   Buenos Aires

For Christina Tugeau, and to Stephen Mooser & Lin Oliver for the "I" in SCBWI.
And very special thanks to Ken Geist, Edie Weinberg, and Melissa Torres — P.B.

Copyright © 2003 by Priscilla Burris. All rights reserved. Published by Scholastic Inc.
SCHOLASTIC, CARTWHEEL BOOKS, and associated logos are trademarks and/or registered trademarks of Scholastic Inc.
Library of Congress Cataloging-in-Publication Data available

ISBN 0-439-35489-7

Book design by Peter Koblish

10 9 8 7 6 5 4 3 2 1   03 04 05 06 07

Printed in China 62
First printing, March 2003
Reinforced Binding for Library Use

Five green and speckled frogs . . .

sat on a speckled log,
    eating some most delicious bugs.

One jumped into the pool,
where it was nice and cool.

Now there are **four** green and speckled frogs.

One jumped into the pool,
    where it was nice and cool.

Now there are **three** green and speckled frogs.

Three green and speckled frogs
sat on a speckled log,
eating some most delicious bugs.

One jumped into the pool,
where it was nice and cool.

Now there are **two** green and speckled frogs.

Two green and speckled frogs
sat on a speckled log,
eating some most delicious bugs.

One jumped into the pool,
where it was nice and cool.

Now there is **one** green and speckled frog.

One lonely speckled frog
sat on a lonely log,
eating some mostly crumpled bugs.

She jumped into the pool,
where it was nice and cool.

Five green and speckled frogs
are having fun!